W9-BTI-036

CARE BEARS™
UNLOCK THE MAGIC

Become our fan on Facebook facebook.com/idwpublishing
Follow us on Twitter @idwpublishing
Subscribe to us on YouTube youtube.com/idwpublishing
See what's new on Tumblr tumblr.idwpublishing.com
Check us out on Instagram instagram.com/idwpublishing

IDW

Series Edits
BOBBY CURNOW
and MEGAN BROWN

Collection Edits
JUSTIN EISINGER
and ALONZO SIMON

Cover Art
AGNES GARBOWSKA

ISBN: 978-1-68405-622-4 **23 22 21 20 1 2 3 4**

Printed in Korea.

IDW Publishing does not read or accept unsolicited submissions of ideas, stories, or artwork.

Originally published as CARE BEARS issues #1–3.

Special thanks to Dara Weiss, Ryan Wiesbrock, Carlos Villagra, and Patricia Phan for their invaluable assistance.

For international rights, contact licensing@idwpublishing.com

WRITTEN BY

MATTHEW ERMAN & NADIA SHAMMAS

ART BY

AGNES GARBOWSKA

COLORS BY

SILVANA BRYS

LETTERS AND DESIGN BY

CHRISTA MIESNER

ART BY **AGNES GARBOWSKA**

HA HA HA HA HA!
ROBBIE! YOU'VE FINALLY DONE IT!

IT WUDN'T NOTHIN', NOT FOR ME! I'M THE BEST AT BEING BAD!

HEH. WELL, SECOND BEST AT BEING BAD! WHICH IS PRETTY BAD CONSIDERIN' I'M NUMBER ONE! ME! BLUSTER!

THIS IS ONE BAD DOODAD, ROBBIE! WITH THIS, WE'LL FINALLY BE ABLE TO SPREAD BLUSTERLAND AS FAR AS THE EYE CAN SEE! WE'RE GUNNA STOP THE WHIFFLES FROM PLANTING ANY MORE OF THOSE SEEDS OF CARING!

THEY WON'T KNOW WHAT HIT 'EM!

MEANWHILE...

IN THE CLOUDSEEKER BATHROOM...
OH GRUMPY, YOU'VE BEEN WORKING NONSTOP. FIXED EVERYTHING ON THIS SHIP AT LEAST TWICE IN THE LAST WEEK! SO TIRED YOU'VE GOT CARE BLISTERS.

NO REASON TO WORRY, THOUGH—TODAY'S OUR DAY OFF! A LITTLE REST AND RELAXATION, TAKING IT EASY. THAT'S THE TICKET...
GRUMPY PLAY! *DIBBLE BORED!*
WELL, ALMOST THE TICKET.

HOW ABOUT WE GO HELP GRUMPY PUT TOGETHER SOME SNACKS? WE HAVE RAINBOW SMOOTHIES, SUGAR-FREE RAINBOW CUPCAKES WITH RAINBOW FROSTING, AND... CELERY STICKS. GREEN CELERY STICKS.
SOUNDS LIKE A PARTY! YOU GOT IT, CHEER! HEY...

BWAAAANG
CRAAASSH
WHAT. IS. THAT?!
BOOOOOOOOOOOOOM

HEY! LET ME SEE WHAT YOU HAVE—
POWER CAREDRIVE!
DIBBLE *NO!!*

DIBBLE PLAY! FUN!
DIBBLE, PLEASE! FOR THE LOVE OF ALL THAT IS GOOD, PLEASE DON'T *BREAK* ANYTHING!
WELL, GUESS WE FOUND OUT WHAT THAT NOISE WAS...

CARE BEARS! WE HAVE AN EMER— OH... WHAT'S GOING ON...? *HAHA!*
HAHAHA! GRUMP! IT'S LOOKING LIKE YOU'RE STARTING TO FINALLY EMBRACE YOUR INNER WHIFFLE! EXCELLENT JOB!

WE WERE JUST ENJOYING THE DOWNTIME, HAVING FUN AND TRYING TO MAKE THE MOST OUT OF A RARE DAY OFF! I THINK WE'VE BEEN *PRETTY SUCCESSFUL* SO FAR!
BUSINESS BAD! GRUMPY PLAY!

WELL! SORRY TO SAY, BUT WE HAVE A NEW ALERT FOR YOU TO INVESTIGATE! IT SEEMS THAT THE OH-SO-ADORABLE WHIFFLES AT THE GLASS GLACIERS NEED YOUR HELP.
THAT'S NO PROBLEM FOR US! THE WHIFFLES ALWAYS COME FIRST.
BEDTIME WILL FILL EVERYONE IN ON THE DETAILS! BEST WISHES, TEAM!

YOU HEARD 'EM, EVERYONE! *TIME TO HEAD OUT!*

POWERING UP THE *RAINBOW CONVERTER* TO *LUDICROUS SPEED!*
LET'S GO!!

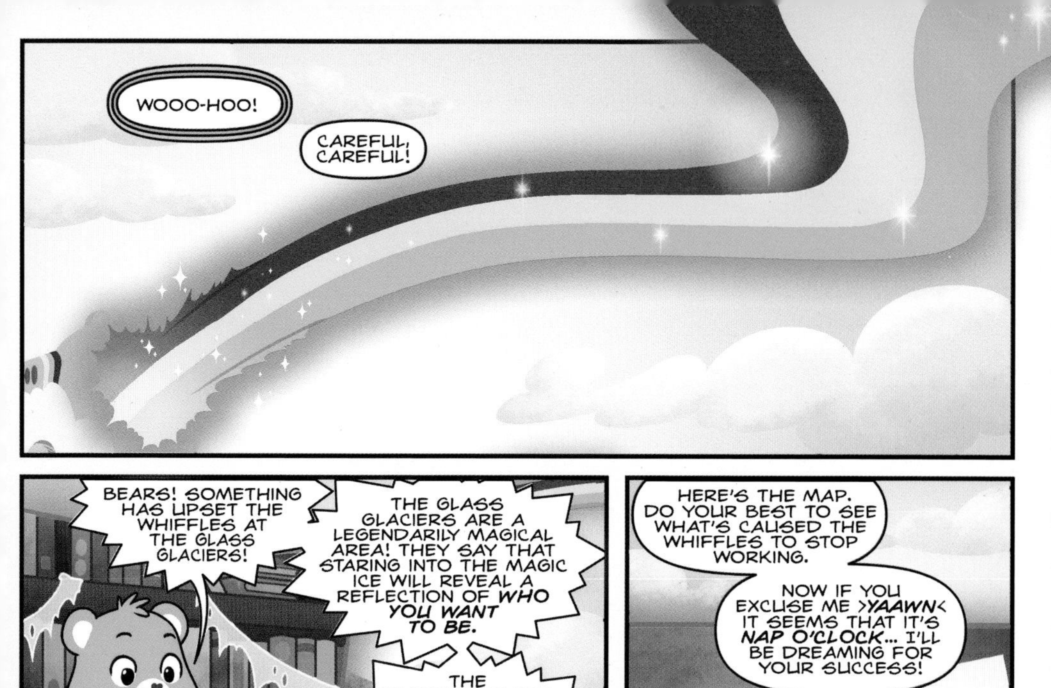
WOOO-HOO!
CAREFUL, CAREFUL!

BEARS! SOMETHING HAS UPSET THE WHIFFLES AT THE GLASS GLACIERS!
THE GLASS GLACIERS ARE A LEGENDARILY MAGICAL AREA! THEY SAY THAT STARING INTO THE MAGIC ICE WILL REVEAL A REFLECTION OF ***WHO YOU WANT TO BE.***
THE WHIFFLES THERE ARE TASKED WITH MAKING SURE THE GLACIERS ARE ALWAYS POLISHED AND SHINY, READY FOR VISITORS.

HERE'S THE MAP. DO YOUR BEST TO SEE WHAT'S CAUSED THE WHIFFLES TO STOP WORKING.
NOW IF YOU EXCUSE ME >***YAAWN***< IT SEEMS THAT IT'S ***NAP O'CLOCK***... I'LL BE DREAMING FOR YOUR SUCCESS!

SOME DAY OFF! I ***WISH*** I COULD HAVE A ***NAP***...
OH, GRUMPY!
THE GLASS GLACIERS

WHOAAAAAAAA, BROO...

IT'S AMAZING! IT'S BEAUTIFUL! IT'S... *REFLECTIVE!*

OKAY! I GUESS WE'RE DOING QUESTIONS. YES, FUNSHINE...?

CAN WE GO LOOK AT THE MIRRORS? *RIGHT NOW?*
YES, AGREED. THAT. THAT SAME QUESTION.

AFTER WE HELP THE WHIFFLES. REMEMBER, IF THE WHIFFLES AREN'T HAPPY, THEY WON'T PLANT AND SOW THE SEEDS OF CARING. AND IF THEY STOP, NEW AREAS OF CARE-A-LOT WON'T GROW IN THE SILVER LINING!

B-BIFFLE SAY N-NO MORE SHINE!
MIFFIE SAY MUST SHINE!
HEY! WE FOUND 'EM! LET'S SEE WHAT THE PROBLEM IS SO WE CAN EXPLORE THIS BEAUTIFUL PLACE.
HELLO THERE! WHAT SEEMS TO BE THE PROBLEM?
G-G-GLACIER REFLECT B-BAD. BIFFLE W-WANT NO REFLECT!
MIFFIE WANT REFLECT!
UH, HELLO?
LOOKS LIKE THEY'RE TOO UPSET TO TALK TO US! WE NEED TO SEPARATE THEM SO WE CAN GET TO THE BOTTOM OF THE PROBLEM.

HELLO, UH ...I'M CHEER BEAR! LEADER OF THE CARE BEARS CLOUDSEEKER TEAM ON A MISSION TO SPREAD GOODNESS AND CARING ALL THROUGH THE SILVER LINING! WHAT'S YOUR NAME?
BUH-BUH-BUH-*BIFFLE* WHIFFLE!
AW, BIFFLE!
IT SEEMS LIKE YOU DON'T WANT THE GLASS GLACIERS TO REFLECT?
WOULD YOU MIND TELLING ME WHY THAT IS?

HI, MIFFIE! IT LOOKS LIKE YOU WANT THESE GLASS GLACIERS TO BE MORE COLORFUL? IS THAT WHY YOU WERE ARGUING?
YES! BIFFLE *STARTED* IT!

MUH-MUH-MUH-MIFFIE AND BIFFLE POLISH AND THEN... MIFFIE SAID M-M-MY *REFLECTION* LOOK *MEAN!*

BIFFLE REFLECTION SAID WE WAS BAD AT WHIFFLEBUMP!

DID NOT!
DID TOO!!

WHAT A MESS! GRUMPY, DO YOU KNOW WHERE DIBBLE IS? MAYBE SHE COULD HELP?
I LOVE DIBBLE, BUT HELPING IS NOT HER STRONG SUIT. ANYWAY, I'VE GOT THIS. GRUMPY TO THE RESCUE!

ALRIGHT, UNCLE GRUMP IS HERE TO SAY, HEY HEY HEY! SO WHEN YOU'RE FEELING BLUE, ALL YOU GOTTA DO IS LOOK TO YOUR FRIEND AND-UHHH... RESP—

LET ME TRY, UNCLE GRUMP...
GOOD TRY THOUGH, BRO!
MIFFIE, ARE YOU SURE YOU HEARD BIFFLE RIGHT?

YEAH! OVER THERE!
HE LOOKED MEAN. BIFFLE MEAN.

MIFFIE MEAN!
AM NOT!

HMMM. "LOOKED MEAN"? BIFFLE'S REFLECTION?
SOMETHING SEEMS OFF ABOUT THIS. I'D BETTER GO INVESTIGATE. SHARE, YOU STAY HERE WITH THE WHIFFLES.

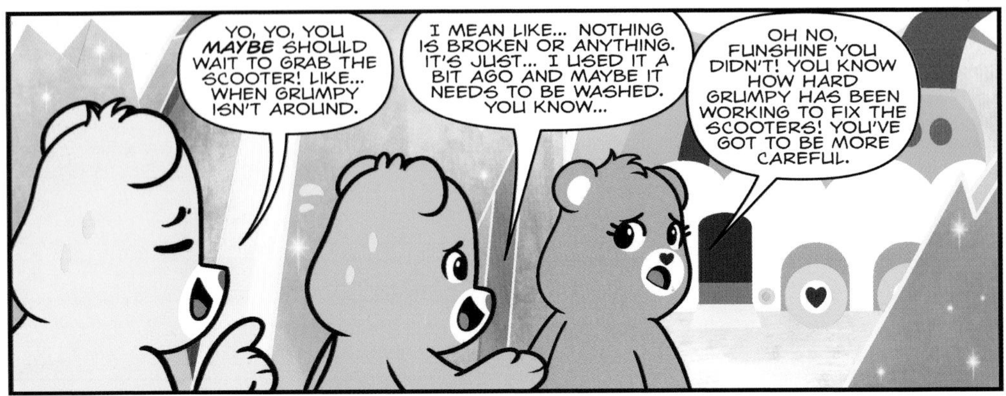
YO, YO, YOU *MAYBE* SHOULD WAIT TO GRAB THE SCOOTER! LIKE... WHEN GRUMPY ISN'T AROUND.
I MEAN LIKE... NOTHING IS BROKEN OR ANYTHING. IT'S JUST... I USED IT A BIT AGO AND MAYBE IT NEEDS TO BE WASHED. YOU KNOW...
OH NO, FUNSHINE YOU DIDN'T! YOU KNOW HOW HARD GRUMPY HAS BEEN WORKING TO FIX THE SCOOTERS! YOU'VE GOT TO BE MORE CAREFUL.

DON'T WORRY, "CAREFUL" IS MY MIDDLE NAME!
WAIT ... I THOUGHT YOUR MIDDLE NAME WAS LUCK?

NEED HELP?

WHOA WHOA WHOA, WHAT HAPPENED! WAS STUNT MAN FUNSHINE OVER HERE TRYING OUT FOR THE CARE-LYMPICS? *LOOK AT THIS THING!*
WELL, UH, IT'S JUST 'CAUSE YOU LOVE FIXING IT SO MUCH! HOW COULD I DENY YOU JOY?

I DON'T FIND JOY IN FI—
HEY! UGH!
COUGH COUGH
CAREFUL!
...THIS IS THE MOST STRESSFUL DAY OFF EVER.

WHOA WHOOA *WHOAAAAAAA!*

WHOA! I LOOK LIKE I COULD TAKE ON *THE WORLD.*

OH! MY TURN TO SHINE! TO *FUN*SHINE!

OH WHOA-HO-HO THIS IS CAPITAL "B" BONKERS! I'M LIKE SOME KIND OF HYPER-AWESOME VERSION OF A CARE BEAR, AND I'VE GOT A TINY SCOOTER!

WHOAAAA!
WHAT DO YOU SEE, GOOD LUCK?!
I SEE...

OH. IT'S JUST ME. I DON'T SEE ANYTHING DIFFERENT.

YOUR TURN, GRUMPY!

NO THANKS, I'VE GOT ENOUGH ON MY HANDS FIXING UP THE SCOOTERS FOR THE BAZILLIONTH TIME.

COME ON, GRUMPY, IT'S JUST A LITTLE BOOST FOR THE MISSION!
I DON'T NEED A MIRROR TO KNOW WHAT I'LL SEE.
ME ON VACATION, WITH CUCUMBERS OVER MY EYES! AND THE LONGER WE TAKE HERE, THE MORE I HAVE TO WAIT FOR OUR DAY OFF TO START!

YOU'RE CRANKY, EVEN FOR YOU, GRUMPMEISTER.
YEAH, EVEN FOR YOU THIS IS EXTRA GROUCHY.
AW, ITS OKAY, GRUMPY. WE'LL BE BACK TO RELAXING SOONER THAN YOU CAN IMAGINE.

HEY, EVERYONE, YOU ALL MIGHT WANT TO SEE THIS!

FUNHOUSE
LEAPIN' RAINBOWS!

BRO, THAT'S THE WILDEST THING I'VE EVER SEEN.
WHERE DID IT COME FROM?

COME ONE, COME ALL, TO THE GREATEST ATTRACTION THIS SIDE OF THE SILVER LINING! IT DELIGHTS, IT FRIGHTS, AND IT'LL KNOCK OUT YOUR LIGHTS, IT'S...
THE NEWEST, BIGGEST, AND BADDEST ATTRACTION EVER FOR A BLUSTERLAND EXPANSION! A LUXURY GLASS GLACIER EXPERIENCE THAT'S ON THE BOUNDARIES OF IMPOSSIBILE! ***BLUSTER'S FUNHOUSE!***

OH... WELL, I GUESS THE BIG MYSTERY IS SOLVED. GREAT, IT'S BLUSTER. WHAT A SURPRISE.
WELL, TEAM, WE'VE STILL GOT TO FIGURE OUT WHAT BLUSTER'S PLAN IS. LET'S BRAINSTORM!

UH, GUYS, WE MIGHT WANT TO PUT A RAINCHECK ON THAT BRAINSTORM...

OH NO! BLUSTER'S FUNHOUSE IS CAUSING THE GLASS GLACIERS TO CRACK. IF WE DON'T DO SOMETHING SOON, THE WHOLE THING COULD SHATTER!

FUNHOUSE
THERE'S NO OTHER WAY, TEAM. IT'S UP TO US AND US ALONE TO SAVE THE DAY FROM WHATEVER BLUSTER IS UP TO!
WE'VE GOT TO GO IN THERE, TRAP OR NOT, AND FLUSH BLUSTER AND HIS BADDIES OUT! ONCE THEY'RE GONE, THE WHIFFLES WILL GO BACK TO MAINTAINING THE GLASS GLACIERS AND NURTURING THEIR SEEDS OF CARING!

LET ME USE MY BELLY BADGE TO CONTACT SHARE— I'M GOING TO FILL HER IN AND LET HER KNOW WHAT WE'RE ABOUT TO DO. HOLD POINT!

OH NO! MY BELLY BADGE IS ACTING UP THANKS TO THE SILVER LINING'S MAGIC! I SURE HOPE SHARE IS DOING ALL RIGHT BY HERSELF...

LOOK WHAT SHARE MADE FOR THE MIFFIE AND BIFFLE! C-CARE CRYSTALS! THEY SMELL LIKE... DIRT! YOU CAN ROLL THEM! ISN'T THAT NEAT? HOW EXCITING! LOOK AT THE FUN I'M HAVING! LOOK!

FUNHOUSE
UHHH—NOT TRYING TO BE NEGATIVE HERE, BUT AREN'T WE WORRIED THAT BLUSTER'S GANG IS WAITING FOR US INSIDE?
OF COURSE! BUT IT'S NOTHING WE CAN'T HANDLE IF WE WORK TOGETHER WITH THE POWER OF FRIENDSHIP!

THIS GLASS DOESN'T LOOK LIKE THE ONES OUTSIDE...

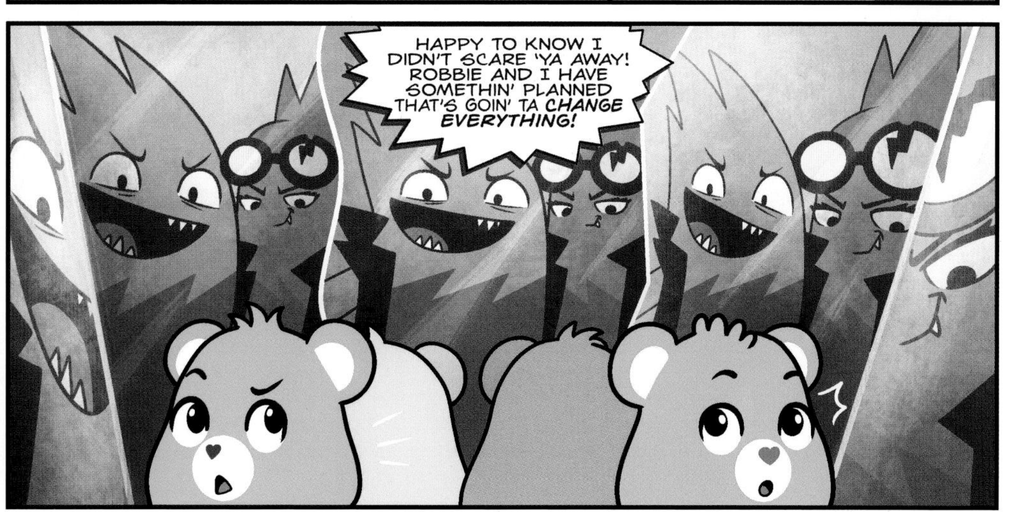
HAPPY TO KNOW I DIDN'T SCARE 'YA AWAY! ROBBIE AND I HAVE SOMETHIN' PLANNED THAT'S GOIN' TA *CHANGE EVERYTHING!*

HOPE YOU'RE ALL COMFY, BECAUSE THERE AIN'T NO LEAVING, AND IF YOU DO, IT WON'T BE THE SAME BEAR THAT CAME IN!

YOU'VE ALL WALKED DIRECTLY INTO MY BEST PLANNED TRAP EVER! I'D WISH YA GOOD LUCK BUT... WELL... I DON'T MEAN IT. SMELL YA LATER!
WHAT'S UP? I HEARD MY NAME. I WASN'T PAYING ATTENTION.

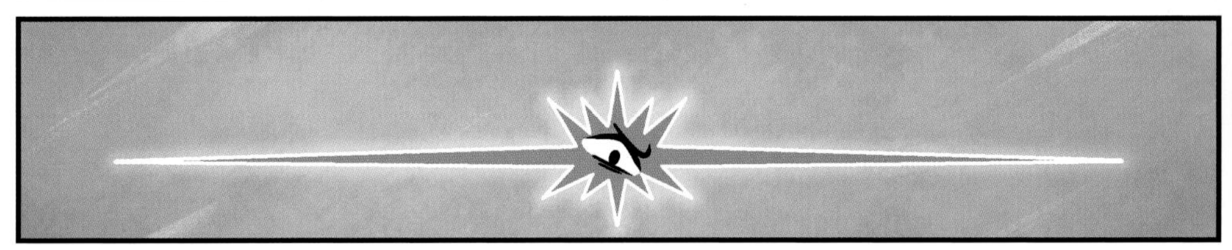

OH, THIS WAS THE TRAP. WE'RE REALLY FIRING ON ALL CYLINDERS TODAY, GUYS. GREAT JOB.

HAVE A LITTLE FAITH, MY DUDE! IT'S NOT LIKE WE'RE LOCKED IN!
KA-CHUNK
KA-CHUNK
NEVERMIND...
HEY... SOMEONE? SOMEONE... ? UHHH... IS ANYONE ELSE SEEING THIS?
WE SEE IT ALL RIGHT...
GRUMPY... YOU MIGHT WANT TO TURN AROUND...
WHAT? ARE YOU GUYS TRYING TO GET ME TO LOOK AT THE MIRRORS AGAIN? I ALREADY TOLD YOU...
NO REALLY, GRUMPY, LOOK!

WWH WH WHHAT??

GRUMPY™
BEAR
FUNSHINE™
BEAR

ART BY **AGNES GARBOWSKA**

SO... UHH—HEH HEH, WHAT WERE YOUR JOBS, EXACTLY?

POLISH THE MIRRORS—MAKE REFLECT PRETTY-PRETTY!!

HZZZ* SHARE! *HZZZ* SOME—ING S—ANGE! *HZZZ* BLUSTER! *HZZZ* MAGIC MIRRORS!!
GOSH DARNIT! MY COMMUNICATOR ISN'T WORKING, AND THE GROUP IS IN TROUBLE! OH... WHAT SHOULD I DO?

NO GOOD! I CAN'T GET THE COMMS TO WORK! WE'LL JUST HAVE TO FIGURE THIS OUT WITHOUT SHARE.
WE CAN DO IT!

I GOTTA BELIEVE THAT SHARE IS TAKING CARE OF THOSE ADORABLE LIL' WHIFFLES AND UHH... THE CLOUDSEEKER.
OH, THE CLOUDSEEKER! I HOPE IT'S DOING OK...
HEY, MY DUDE, I KNOW WE BROACHED THIS EARLIER BUT... YOUR REFLECTION IS EVEN WONKIER.
WHA-HUH?!

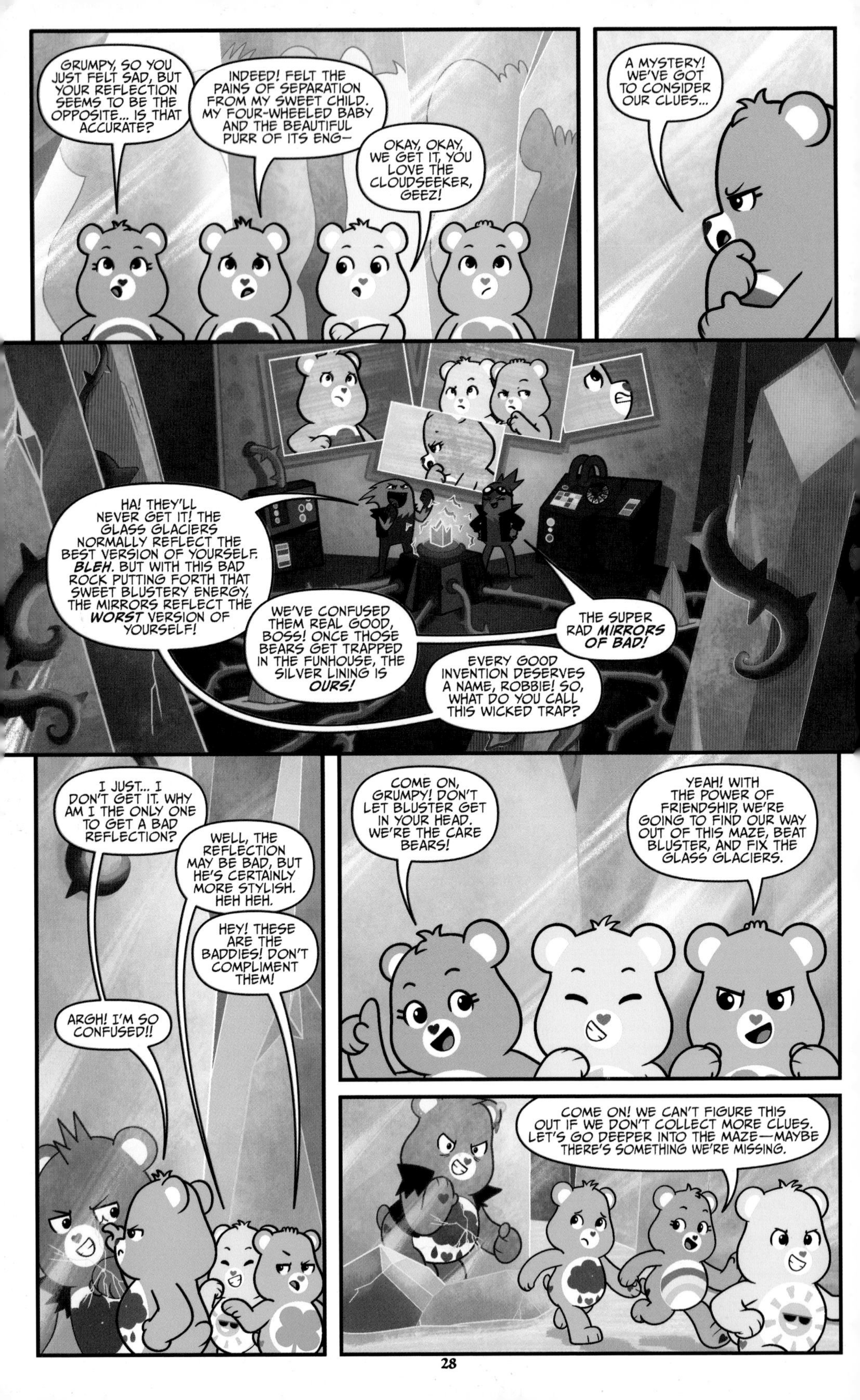
GRUMPY, SO YOU JUST FELT SAD, BUT YOUR REFLECTION SEEMS TO BE THE OPPOSITE... IS THAT ACCURATE?
INDEED! FELT THE PAINS OF SEPARATION FROM MY SWEET CHILD. MY FOUR-WHEELED BABY AND THE BEAUTIFUL PURR OF ITS ENG—
OKAY, OKAY, WE GET IT, YOU LOVE THE CLOUDSEEKER, GEEZ!
A MYSTERY! WE'VE GOT TO CONSIDER OUR CLUES...
HA! THEY'LL NEVER GET IT! THE GLASS GLACIERS NORMALLY REFLECT THE BEST VERSION OF YOURSELF. BLEH. BUT WITH THIS BAD ROCK PUTTING FORTH THAT SWEET BLUSTERY ENERGY, THE MIRRORS REFLECT THE WORST VERSION OF YOURSELF!
WE'VE CONFUSED THEM REAL GOOD, BOSS! ONCE THOSE BEARS GET TRAPPED IN THE FUNHOUSE, THE SILVER LINING IS OURS!
EVERY GOOD INVENTION DESERVES A NAME, ROBBIE! SO, WHAT DO YOU CALL THIS WICKED TRAP?
THE SUPER RAD MIRRORS OF BAD!
I JUST... I DON'T GET IT. WHY AM I THE ONLY ONE TO GET A BAD REFLECTION?
WELL, THE REFLECTION MAY BE BAD, BUT HE'S CERTAINLY MORE STYLISH. HEH HEH.
HEY! THESE ARE THE BADDIES! DON'T COMPLIMENT THEM!
ARGH! I'M SO CONFUSED!!
COME ON, GRUMPY! DON'T LET BLUSTER GET IN YOUR HEAD. WE'RE THE CARE BEARS!
YEAH! WITH THE POWER OF FRIENDSHIP, WE'RE GOING TO FIND OUR WAY OUT OF THIS MAZE, BEAT BLUSTER, AND FIX THE GLASS GLACIERS.
COME ON! WE CAN'T FIGURE THIS OUT IF WE DON'T COLLECT MORE CLUES. LET'S GO DEEPER INTO THE MAZE—MAYBE THERE'S SOMETHING WE'RE MISSING.

HEY, WHERE DO THEY THINK THEY'RE GOING!
IF WE KNOW THE CARE BEARS...
AND WE DO.
THEN THEY'RE UP TO SOMETHING! YOU CAN BET ON IT!
GREAT OBSERVATION, ROBBIE. YOU'RE REALLY PROVING YOURSELF AS MY NUMBER 2! TIME TO TURN UP THE BADNESS!
THIS OUTTA DO IT...
BOSS!
I'M NOT YOUR BOSS, ROBBIE. BOSSES AREN'T COOL. I'M YOUR... OVERLORD. CALL ME THAT.
YOU GOT IT... *OVERLORD!*

UH-OH... THIS MIGHT NOT BE AS EASY AS WE THOUGHT...
DID WE GET TURNED AROUND? ARE WE LOST?!
BOY OH BOY, OUR DAY OFF KEEPS GETTING BETTER...
JUST MY LUCK!
DEADEND
TO CENTER
to CENTER
to CENTER
DEADEND

BLUSTER! YOU CAN'T SPOOK ME WITH YOUR TRICKS AND GOOFS! I *KNOW* WHO I AM, AND NO MATTER WHAT MY REFLECTION LOOKS LIKE, MY TEAM DEPENDS ON ME TO KEEP A LEVEL HEAD AND KIND HEART!

OH, SO LITTLE MISS GOOD VIBES HERE THINKS SHE CAN BEAT THE BADDIES? WELL, LET'S HIT CHEER BEAR WHERE IT HURTS! IN HER *FEELINGS.*

GUYS...?

EVERYONE...? WHERE DID YOU ALL GO?

BOO.

I KNOW YOU'RE A TRICK! YOU'RE NOT REAL! YOU'RE JUST A—

DON'T WORRY BO—I MEAN OVERLORD. I'VE GOT THIS UNDER CONTROL.
HOW SO, MY DEVIOUS HENCHPERSON?
OH, YOU'LL SEE...

OH, CHEER! HOW CAN YOU BE SO SURE I'M NOT REAL? WOULD YOU BE WILLING TO RISK YOUR MISSION ON IT? RISK THE SILVER LINING? RISK... CARE-A-LOT?

I'D NEVER RISK MY FRIENDS! THAT'S JUST ONE OF THE WAYS YOU AND I ARE DIFFERENT, AND HOW I *KNOW* YOU'RE NOT THE REAL THING!

WELL, YOU KNOW WHAT THEY SAY: THE ONLY THING TO FEAR IS...

FEAR *ITSELF*!

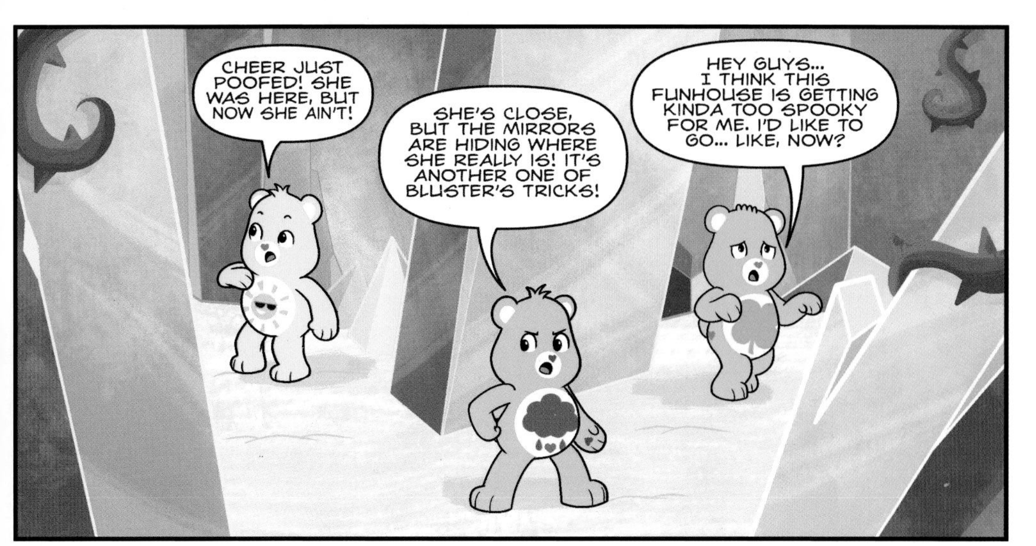
CHEER JUST POOFED! SHE WAS HERE, BUT NOW SHE AIN'T!
SHE'S CLOSE, BUT THE MIRRORS ARE HIDING WHERE SHE REALLY IS! IT'S ANOTHER ONE OF BLUSTER'S TRICKS!
HEY GUYS... I THINK THIS FUNHOUSE IS GETTING KINDA TOO SPOOKY FOR ME. I'D LIKE TO GO... LIKE, NOW?

HEY, WHAT UP VIEWERS, IT'S YA BOI G.L.B. HERE, DON'T FORGET TO *SMASH* THAT LIKE AND SUBSCRIBE BUTTON! WE'RE HERE IN THE SILVER LINING ABOUT TO EM-*BEAR*-AS THESE UNCOOL BEARS.
...UHHHH WHAT'S GOING ON?

DAB!
YOU'RE NOT SUPPOSED TO SAY IT WHEN YOU DO IT! UGH! YOU'RE SO *UNCOOL!* YOU'RE NOWHERE NEAR AS COOL AS I AM!

REAL RIPE COMING FROM SOMEONE AS UNCOOL AS *YOU*. YOU DON'T EVEN HAVE TO WORK HARD TO WIN, YOU JUST RELY ON YOUR LUCK!
WHO ARE YOU TALKING TO?!
HAHAHA, *YOU*, LOSER!

OH, COME ON! NOW *I'M* LOST?! WHAT GIVES?!
YO! I THOUGHT YOU GOT LOST, DUDE. COME ON, WE'VE GOTTA STICK TOGETHER, OTHERWISE WE'LL REALLY GET LO–
LOST?
OH, YOU'RE ALREADY LOST... THAT'S SO SAD!
WHOA, YOU LOOK JUST LIKE ME! BUT... LIKE—REALLY SAD! WHAT GIVES?!
OH, MAN... BRO, IT'S COOL—DON'T CRY OVER SPILLED MILK.
B-B-BUT... I ***HATE*** MILK...
THIS IS GONNA BE A TOUGH ONE!

OH, CHEER! ALL YOU'VE EVER WANTED IS ADVENTURE. YOU'RE A LEADER ON A MISSION, BUT ISN'T YOUR DREAM TO EXPLORE ALL OF THE SILVER LINING?
I... I... I'M THE LEADER OF THE CLOUDSEEKER TEAM! I'D NEVER TURN MY BACK ON MY FRIENDS!
LEADER? A GREAT LEADER LIKE YOU WOULD NEVER LEAD YOUR TEAM INTO A TRAP, RIGHT? A GREAT LEADER WOULD NEVER LEAVE YOUR TEAM BEHIND IN THE MAZE, CORRECT? A GREAT LEADER WOULD NEVER... QUESTION THEIR DECISIONS! CHEER, MY GIRL—YOU'RE A BAD LEADER!
NO! THAT'S NOT TRUE!
YOU CARE MORE ABOUT THRILLS THAN YOUR FRIENDS' SAFETY!
IN FACT, MAYBE YOU SHOULD JUST COME ON OVER TO THE BAD SIDE! BLUSTER IS A PRETTY GREAT BOSS...
NO! CALL HIM YOUR OVERLORD!
—I MEAN OVERLORD, AND IF YOU REALLY WANT TO INDULGE YOUR LEADERSHIP AND YOUR TASTE FOR ADVENTURE, JOIN THE BAD CROWD AND HELP SPREAD CHAOS THROUGH THE SILVER LINING!
CHEER, YOU CAN DO THIS.
I CAN'T DISAPPOINT MY FRIENDS! I'VE GOT TO BE...
CHEERFUL!

YOU'RE WRONG, FEAR! I'M A GOOD LEADER NOT BECAUSE I TAKE RISKS BUT BECAUSE MY TEAM—NO, MY FRIENDS—GRUMPY, FUNSHINE, GOOD LUCK AND SHARE, TRUST ME!
HSSSSSSS—NO! HOW ARE YOU SO CONFIDENT?!
MY FRIENDS BELIEVE IN ME! THEY BELIEVE THAT I CAN LEAD THEM TO VICTORY! LEAD THEM THROUGH HARD TIMES! LEAD THEM THROUGH ANYTHING! YOU WON'T BE AFRAID IF YOU HAVE FRIENDS THAT CARE FOR YOU, THAT FIGHT FOR YOU—THAT GIVE YOU...
COURAGE!!!!
NO! NO! BE AFRAID! BE VERY AFRAID!!
KRRSHHAAABBOOOMM

WHAT... IT'S JUST ONE OF BLUSTER'S CRONIES IN A SUIT!

UH-OH, THE BOSS AIN'T GONNA BE HAPPY ABOUT THIS...
TIME TO SCRAM!

IF THESE MIRRORS ARE MEANT TO TRICK US INTO LOSING FAITH IN OURSELVES...

I'VE GOT TO FIND MY FRIENDS!

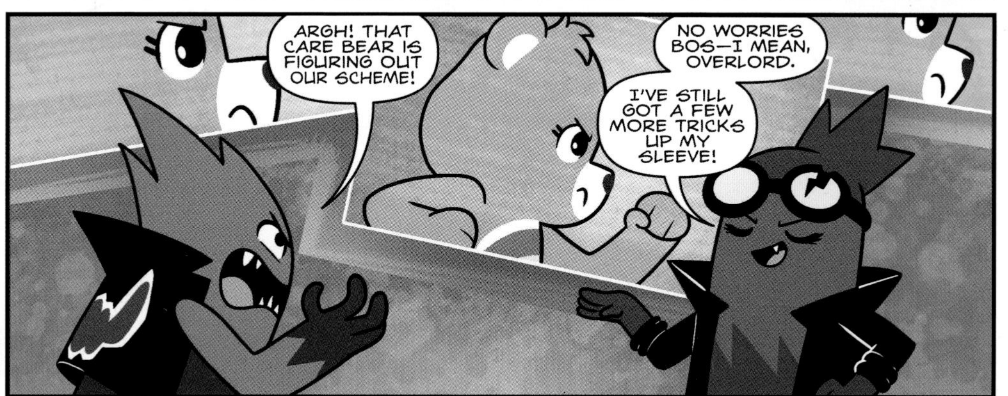
ARGH! THAT CARE BEAR IS FIGURING OUT OUR SCHEME!
NO WORRIES BOS—I MEAN, OVERLORD.
I'VE STILL GOT A FEW MORE TRICKS UP MY SLEEVE!

G.L.B. HERE WITH THE 4-1-1 ON THE HOTTEST *PRANKS* AROUND. THIS WEEK, WE'RE DOING THE "THROW DIRT ON PEOPLE'S NICE SHOES" PRANK!
THAT'S NOT EVEN A REAL *PRANK*, THAT'S JUST MEAN!
LOOKS LIKE WE'VE GOT A HATER HERE, FAMSQUAD!
NO COMPARISON, BRO. THE CAMERA DON'T LIE.
I'VE GOT STYLE, I'VE GOT LOOKS. I STUNT ON EVERYBODY WITH THESE THREADS! YOU'VE GOT *NOTHING*.

IT'S NO SWEAT, BRO. YOU'RE NOT *TOTALLY* UNCOOL.
IF YOU JOIN BLUSTER'S GANG, IT'D BE SO LIT. THE HOTTEST TRENDS BRO, *FIRE!* FOLLOWERS BY THE THOUSANDS.

WHO NEEDS A FEW UNCOOL FRIENDS WHEN YOU COULD HAVE *FANS?*

YOU'RE WRONG! MAKING PEOPLE FEEL BAD AND WEARING EXPENSIVE CLOTHES DOSEN'T MAKE YOU COOL.
HAVING FRIENDS YOU CARE ABOUT AND BEING NICE IS COOL. MAKING PEOPLE FEEL GOOD IS COOL!

I MIGHT CARE TOO MUCH ABOUT MY LOOKS SOMETIMES, BUT I KNOW YOU'RE NOT THE REAL ME BECAUSE I'D ***NEVER*** MAKE A JOKE OUT OF MY FRIENDS. IT'S NOT ***FUNNY***.

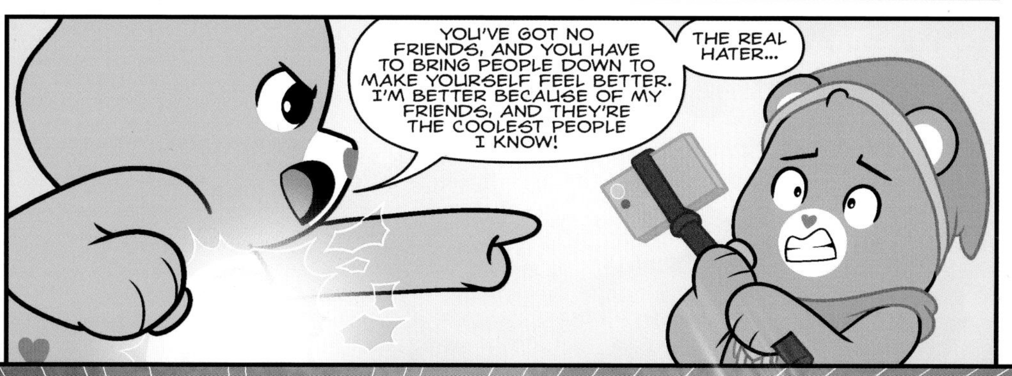
YOU'VE GOT NO FRIENDS, AND YOU HAVE TO BRING PEOPLE DOWN TO MAKE YOURSELF FEEL BETTER. I'M BETTER BECAUSE OF MY FRIENDS, AND THEY'RE THE COOLEST PEOPLE I KNOW!
THE REAL HATER...

...IS YOU!
NOOOO, BROOOOOO!

WHOA...
I GOTTA GET OUTTA HERE!

WELL, THAT WAS WEIRD.
WAIT, IF THAT GUY WAS TRYING TO PRY US APART AND RECRUIT US TO THE BAD CROWD... THEN THAT MEANS...

CHEER! GRUMPY!
FUNSHINE! HANG IN THERE, BRO, I'M COMING!

HEY, HEY, IT'S OKAY! NO NEED TO CRY!

LOOKIE HERE. WHENEVER I'M FEELING DIGGITY-DOWN, I JUST DO A LITTLE ***CARE BEAR SHUFFLE!*** COME ON, GIVE IT A TRY!

OH YEAH, FEEL IT!

YEAH! LET THE MUSIC TAKE YOU! FEEL THE HEART OF THE GROOVE!

WAAAAAA, I CAN'T DO IT!
WHOA, I'M SORRY.

COME ON, BUDDY, HELP ME OUT HERE. WHAT KIND OF REFLECTION ARE YOU?
I'M... I'M YOUR REAL REFLECTION.

WHAAAAT?!

DON'T YOU SEE? I'M THE REAL YOU. WHY DO YOU THINK YOU'RE SO CHEERFUL ALL THE TIME? IT'S BECAUSE YOU'RE HIDING YOUR REAL FEELINGS.
THAT MAKES NO SENSE, BRO.
WHEN YOU HANG AROUND THE OTHER CARE BEARS, THEY DON'T APPRECIATE YOUR JOKES AND YOUR ANTICS. THEY JUST WANT YOU TO BE FUN, BUT NOT TOO FUN.
THAT'S NOT...
WHY DON'T YOU JOIN THE BAD CROWD? THEY'LL LET YOU BE WHOEVER YOU WANNA BE! BREAK WHATEVER YOU WANT! NOT LIKE THOSE OTHER CARE BEARS.
HAHAHA!
WAAAAA! WHY ARE YOU LAUGHING?!
BECAUSE THAT'S JUST SILLY, BRO! MY FRIENDS LOVE ME FOR ME. I DANCE AND JOKE AROUND BECAUSE I WANT TO MAKE MY FRIENDS HAPPY, NOT BECAUSE I'M HIDING ANYTHING!
NO MATTER WHAT YOU SAY...
YOU'LL NEVER DIM MY SHINE!
WAAAAA!

WHOA...

I BETTER GO FIND THE OTHERS! THEY MIGHT NEED MY HELP!

GRUMPY? GOOD LUCK??

CHEER? FUNSHINE?? BRO, WHERE ARE YOU!!

GRUMPY? CHEEEEER??

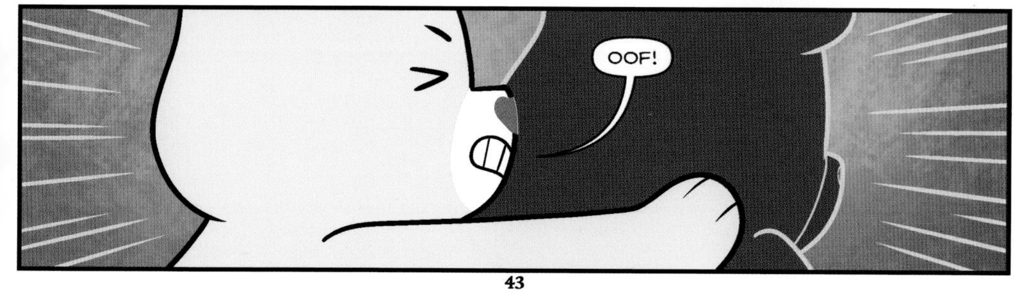
OOF!

WE MADE IT!
ALL RIGHT!! I KNEW WE'D BE FINE!

HEY, GUYS... WHERE'S GRUMPY?

OH, NO! WE HAVE TO FIND HIM!

SHOULD WE SPLIT UP?
NO! GRUMPY MIGHT NEED OUR HELP, SO WE'VE ALL GOTTA STICK TOGETHER!

GRRRLLLLLLLMMMPPPPYYYY?

GRUMPSTER? GRUMP-MAN!
HELLO?

GRUMPY??

WHAT'S WRONG?
WHOA!

DON'T RECOGNIZE YOUR GOOD FRIEND, GRUMPY?
HAHA!

SHARE™
BEAR
BEDTIME™
BEAR
GOOD LUCK™
BEAR

ART BY **AGNES GARBOWSKA**

SEVERAL WEEKS AGO...
"SEE, WHAT BLUSTER FOUND WAS SOMETHING UNBELIEVABLE. THE ROCK OF REFLECTION."
HEY-O! ROBBIE! MINION! I'M THINKIN' MY SUPER SPECIAL TECHNIQUE HAS UNEARTHED SOMETHING STRANGE. SOMETHING... BAD AND RAD. LET'S CALL IT... BADICAL.
HEH-HEH! I KNEW YOU COULD DO IT, BLUSTER! IF THERE'S ONE THING A ROBBIE IS GOOD FOR IT'S BELIEVIN' IN THE BADDEST GUY AROUND.

YUCK. YOU'RE STARTIN' TO SOUND A LOT LIKE THOSE GOODY-TWO-PAWS CARE BEARS. GEEZ, WHAT I COULDN'T GIVE TO CLOWN ON THOSE GOOFBALLS. THEY'RE SOO...
CARING!

"HE DIDN'T KNOW WHAT IT DID, BUT HE HANDED IT OVER TO ME AND TOLD ME TO GET TO WORK ON SOMETHING SO BLUSTERY IT'D MAKE MY HEAD SPIN.

"HIS PLAN WAS UNDERWAY AND UNSTOPPABLE. THANKS TO ME..."

HEY. WHY ARE YOU TELLING MY MASTER PLA—

BLUSTER'S MASTER PLA—!
OH-OW!
IXNAY ON THE USTERBLAY...!
IT WAS -MY- MASTER PLAN!!
ALL BECAUSE OF MY TINKERING AND TAMPERING!! NOW THAT DOOFUS, GRUMPY, HAS SWITCHED SIDES TO BECOME THE NEWEST MEMBER OF THE BAD CROWD!
BWHA HA HAHA HA HAH!

HEY! THAT'S NOT GRUMPY! WE ALREADY FIGURED OUT EVERYTHING. IT'S NOT A MYSTERY ANYMORE!
YEAH! WE CRACKED THE CASE ON THE OTHER CARE BEAR IMPOSTERS AND NOW...
OH. UHHH. YEAH! EVERYTHING THEY SAID BUT NOW I'M SAYING IT!!

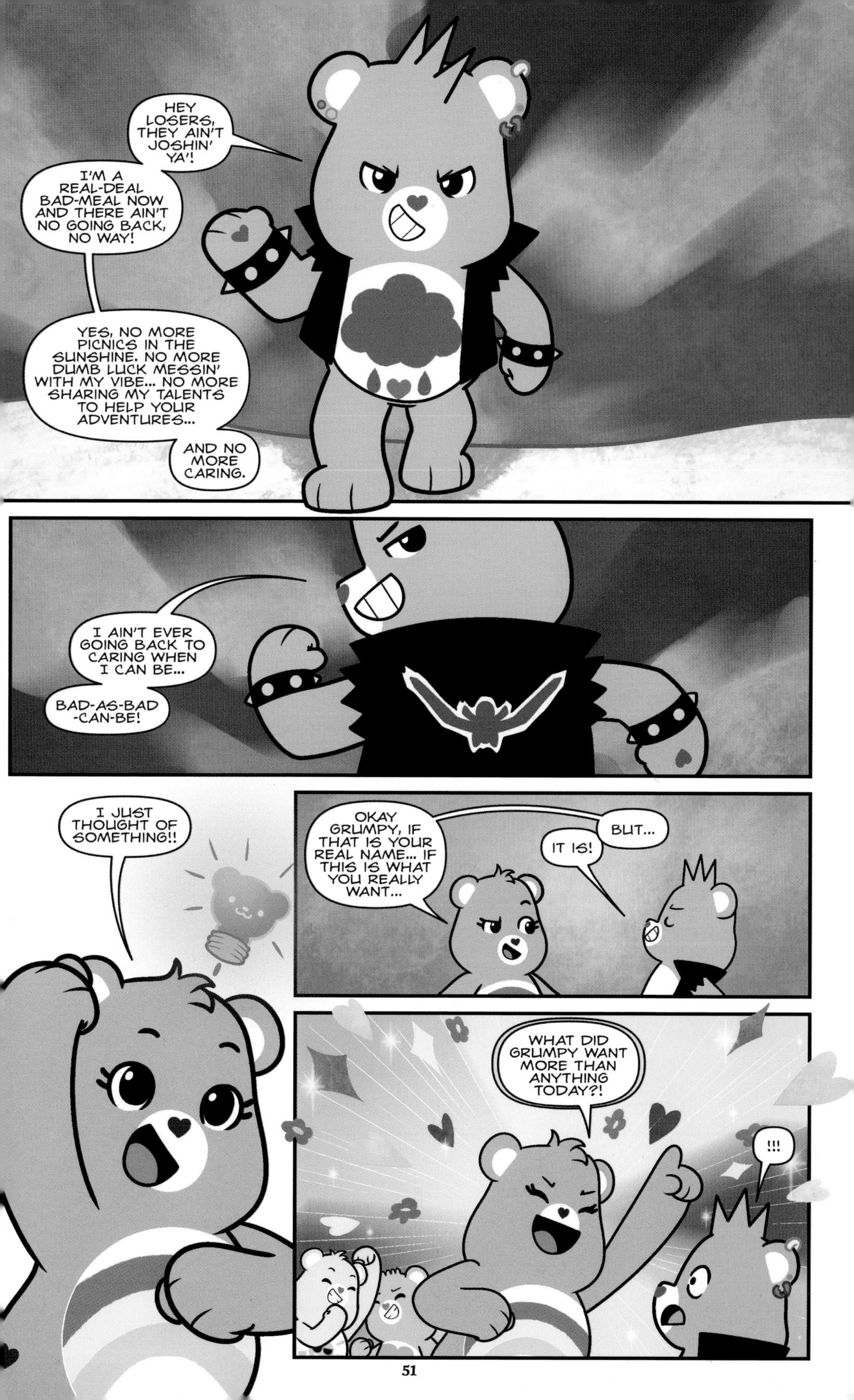
HEY LOSERS, THEY AIN'T JOSHIN' YA'!
I'M A REAL-DEAL BAD-MEAL NOW AND THERE AIN'T NO GOING BACK, NO WAY!
YES, NO MORE PICNICS IN THE SUNSHINE. NO MORE DUMB LUCK MESSIN' WITH MY VIBE... NO MORE SHARING MY TALENTS TO HELP YOUR ADVENTURES...
AND NO MORE CARING.
I AIN'T EVER GOING BACK TO CARING WHEN I CAN BE...
BAD-AS-BAD -CAN-BE!
OKAY GRUMPY, IF THAT IS YOUR REAL NAME... IF THIS IS WHAT YOU REALLY WANT...
IT IS!
BUT...
I JUST THOUGHT OF SOMETHING!!
WHAT DID GRUMPY WANT MORE THAN ANYTHING TODAY?!
!!!

I... UHH... GRUMPY... HE- I MEAN I- I WANTED TO... GLOWER AT... UHH... THE WHIFFLES?
WRONG! GUESS AGAIN!
FIX THE CARE... SCOOTEY?
YOU HATE DOING THAT!
MAKE... SMOOTHIES?
THAT NEVER WORKS OUT AND YOU STOPPED DOING IT BECAUSE OF THE MESS!

AND THAT'S BECAUSE...
YOU'RE NOT GRUMPY!!

GRUMPY IS STILL BACK IN THE MAZE! TRAPPED! I'LL FIND HIM IF YOU TWO WATCH OVER THIS GRUMP-POSTER!

FUNHOUSE
SO WHAT HAPPENS NEXT, ARE YOU GOING TO PUT US IN CARE BEARS JAIL?
JAIL?! ...WHO DO YOU THINK WE ARE?

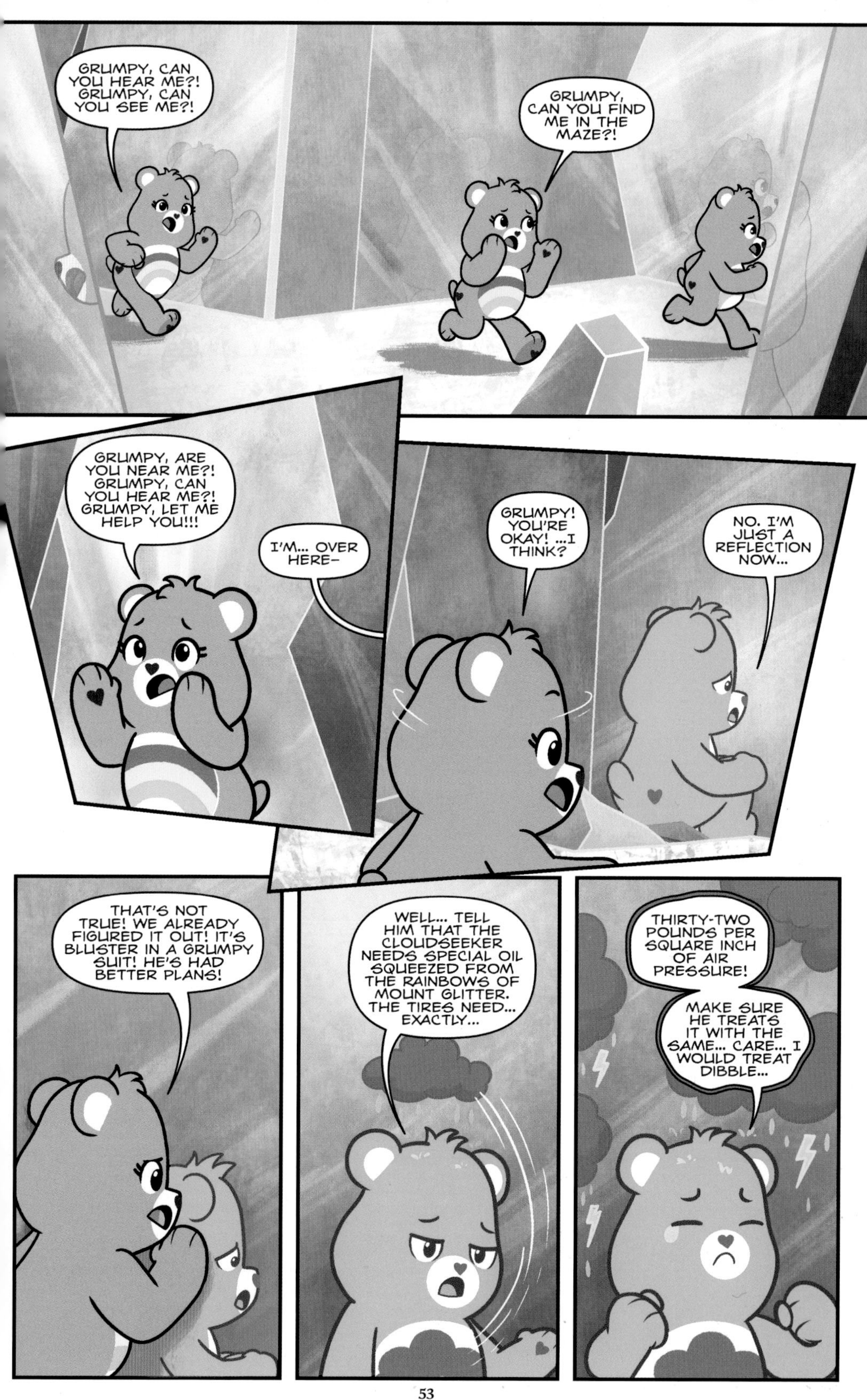
GRUMPY, CAN YOU HEAR ME?! GRUMPY, CAN YOU SEE ME?!
GRUMPY, CAN YOU FIND ME IN THE MAZE?!
GRUMPY, ARE YOU NEAR ME?! GRUMPY, CAN YOU HEAR ME?! GRUMPY, LET ME HELP YOU!!!
I'M... OVER HERE-
GRUMPY! YOU'RE OKAY! ...I THINK?
NO. I'M JUST A REFLECTION NOW...
THAT'S NOT TRUE! WE ALREADY FIGURED IT OUT! IT'S BLUSTER IN A GRUMPY SUIT! HE'S HAD BETTER PLANS!
WELL... TELL HIM THAT THE CLOUDSEEKER NEEDS SPECIAL OIL SQUEEZED FROM THE RAINBOWS OF MOUNT GLITTER. THE TIRES NEED... EXACTLY...
THIRTY-TWO POUNDS PER SQUARE INCH OF AIR PRESSURE!
MAKE SURE HE TREATS IT WITH THE SAME... CARE... I WOULD TREAT DIBBLE...

GRUMPY! I DON'T UNDERSTAND HOW YOU FEEL, BUT... THAT'S OKAY! I'M NOT GRUMPY AND I WON'T EVER BE A GRUMPY BEAR– BUT THAT DOESN'T MEAN WE CAN'T BE HERE FOR YOU AS YOU WORK IT OUT!
THAT'S BECAUSE WE LOVE YOU! ALL THE CARE BEARS!
YOU'RE THE BESTEST FRIEND A BEAR COULD ASK FOR BECAUSE EVEN IF YOU HAVE YOUR BAD DAYS...
YOU STILL CARE!!
ZA-BOOOOOOSH

THAT'S RIGHT, GRUMPY! FEEL HOW MUCH WE CARE ABOUT YOU! I KNOW YOU'RE REALLY YOU! I BELIEVE IT!!

YOU'RE RIGHT! I FEEL SOMETHING!

I FEEL-

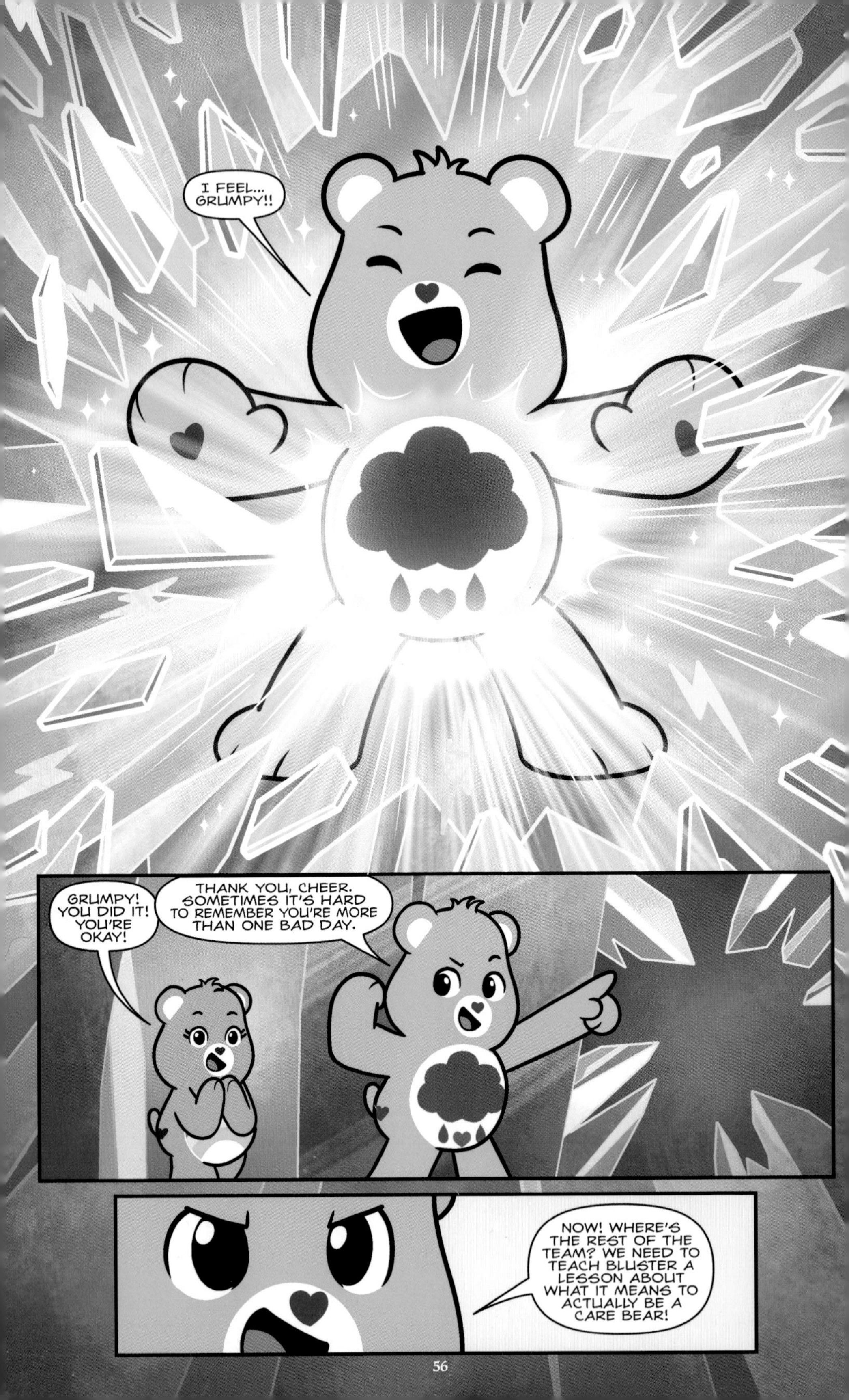
I FEEL... GRUMPY!!
GRUMPY! YOU DID IT! YOU'RE OKAY!
THANK YOU, CHEER. SOMETIMES IT'S HARD TO REMEMBER YOU'RE MORE THAN ONE BAD DAY.
NOW! WHERE'S THE REST OF THE TEAM? WE NEED TO TEACH BLUSTER A LESSON ABOUT WHAT IT MEANS TO ACTUALLY BE A CARE BEAR!

HEY! NO FAIR! WHAT DID YOU GUYS DO TO MY- I MEAN BLUSTER'S CRAZY COOL AND SUPER BADICAL FUNHOUSE?
WE ALREADY KNOW IT'S YOU, BLUSTER!
WHAT'S HAPPENING?!?
OH, NO WAY! IT LOOKS LIKE...
FUNHOUSE
YO! THEY DID IT!
GRUMPY! CHEER! I NEVER DOUBTED YOU FOR A SECOND!

FUNHOUS
OH! OH, YOU ALL RUINED IT! MY TOTALLY RIGHTEOUSLY BAD FUNHOUSE THAT WOULD HAVE SPREAD THROUGHOUT THE SILVER LINING?! HOW?!

WHAT THE BLUSTER?! THEY... THEY... THEY CHANGED MY MAGIC ROCK! IT'S ALL... GROSS AND CUTE! EVERYTHING IS DIFFERENT! EVEN YOU, BLUSTER!!

OH, MAN! NOOOOO! I'M SO... UNCOOL. GET THIS MIRROR SUIT OFF ME!!

I... I... I DON'T KNOW WHAT TO SAY, BOSS! YOU'RE HONESTLY KINDA... ADORABLE! IT'S TERRIBLE!

ME?... ADORABLE!? NO! THAT'S LAME! NOT COOL OR BAD OR RAD OR ANY OF MY FAVORITE WORDS! WHERE'S MY HAIR POMADE?
SOMEONE GET ME MY BAD SEED!!!!
B-B-BLUSTER..? YOU DON'T LOOK SO GOOD...

I'M NOT SUPPOSED TO BE ADORABLE!! I'M MEAN AND BAD. OUTRAGEOUSLY TOO-COOL-FOR-SCHOOL! I'VE GOT 'TUDE IN MY BONES AND YOU CAN'T DEN-

WHAT THE-

CURSES!! CUUUURRRSSSESSS!! WE'LL GET YOU NEXT TIME, CARE BEAAAAARSS!!

WOW. WHAT A MESS.
IT'S GOING TO TAKE FOREVER TO CLEAN THIS UP!
NOT IF WE WORK TOGETHER!

WELCOME BACK, GRUMPY.
YOU'RE THE MAN, GRUMPSTER!
THANKS FOR BELIEVING IN ME, GUYS. EVEN WHEN I DIDN'T BELIEVE IN MYSELF.

ALRIGHT, TEAM! LET'S USE THIS TO FIX UP THE GLASS GLACIERS AND SET EVERYTHING RIGHT!

YEAH, I BET SHARE IS AT HER WIT'S END.

SHARE! I ALMOST FORGOT!!

OOOOOOH, I NEED A NAP.
NAPS BORING!
SHARE! SHARE!!

WHERE WERE YOU?? I GOT SO WORRIED!
WE'RE SO SORRY! IT'S A LONG STORY BUT-
LET ME GUESS. BLUSTER?
OH. YES ACTUALLY. BLUSTER. YOU PRETTY MUCH NAILED IT.
ANYWAY, HOW'S THE WHIFFLES?

WELL- I HAVEN'T QUITE FIGURED OUT HOW TO CHEER THEM UP...

WAIT! I GOT IT!

FUNHOUSE
BIFFLE, MIFFIE, THIS IS WHERE YOU TWO SAW THE BAD REFLECTIONS, RIGHT?
YEAH, BIFFLE MIRROR BAD!
NO, MIFFIE MIRROR BAD!

WHY DON'T YOU TWO GO LOOK ONE MORE TIME?

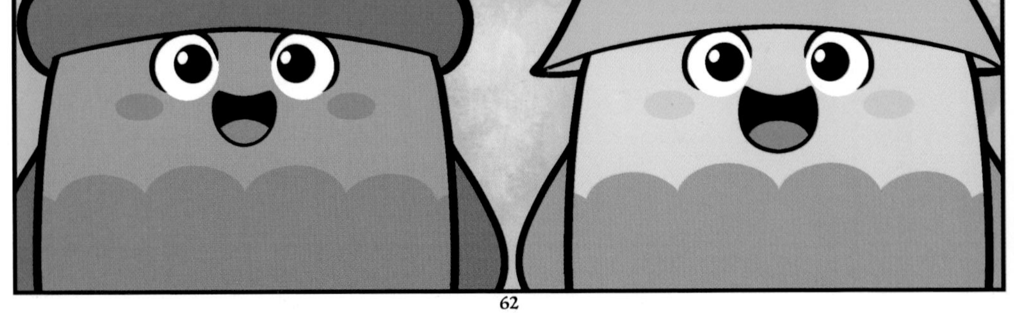

DON'T YOU SEE? THE BEST VERSION OF YOURSELVES... THE REAL VERSIONS OF YOU LITTLE GOOFS...

...ARE BEST FRIENDS!

MIFFIE!
BIFFLE!

GRUMPY! YOU DID IT!
GREAT JOB, UNCLE GRUMP.

HEY GUYS, LOOK!
THE WHIFFLES ARE FIXING THE MIRRORS!

WELL, I THINK WE CAN CALL THIS MISSION A SUCCESS! IT'S TIME TO HEAD BACK TO THE CLOUDSEEKER AND SEND THE MISSION REPORT BACK TO HOME BASE!

...

I MISSED YOU, OLD FRIEND.

WELL, BEFORE YOU PUT THOSE AWAY, LET ME TAKE A LOOK AT THEM. GOTTA BE READY FOR THE NEXT MISSION!

SCOOTERS? NAH. BUD.
WE'VE GOT THE SCOOTERS THIS TIME. PROMISE.
BUT–

WE'VE ONLY GOT ONE MISSION FOR TODAY, CARE BEARS...

IT'S OUR DAY OFF!!
I EVEN ADDED A NEW SOUVENIR! A TINY PIECE OF THE GLASS FROM BLUSTER'S FUNHOUSE! NOW WHEREVER YOU GO, YOU'LL ALWAYS KNOW WHO YOU REALLY ARE!

REALLY??
YUP! IT'S OUR MOST URGENT MISSION YET!

ALRIGHT, CARE BEARS. OFF TO RELAXATION!
WOOHOO!
ALRIGHT!

GRUUUUMPY! WE'RE HEADING OUT!

COMING!

GREETINGS FROM THE SILVER LINING!
WISH YOU WERE HERE!!

SHARE™
BEAR

TENDERHEART™
BEAR

ART BY **TONY FLEECS**

ART BY **NICO PENA** COLORS BY **SILVANA BRYS**

ART BY **MUFFY LEVY**